*B7.CCV.607*

# STAR WARS REBELS™

# SABINE'S
## ART ATTACK

ADAPTED BY JENNIFER HEDDLE

BASED ON THE EPISODE "ART ATTACK,"
WRITTEN BY GREG WEISMAN

ᴅɪꜱɴᴇʏ

**LUCASFILM**
P R E S S

LOS ANGELES • NEW YORK

SANTA CLARA CITY LIBRARY
ABDO
Spotlight
DISCARD
Santa Clara, CA 95051

**ABDOPUBLISHING.COM**

Reinforced library bound edition published in 2016 by Spotlight, a division of ABDO
PO Box 398166, Minneapolis, Minnesota 55439. Spotlight produces high-quality
reinforced library bound editions for schools and libraries.
Published by Disney • Lucasfilm Press, an imprint of Disney Book Group.

Printed in the United States of America, North Mankato, Minnesota.
042015
092015

THIS BOOK CONTAINS
RECYCLED MATERIALS

© & TM 2015 Lucasfilm Ltd.
Published by Disney • Lucasfilm Press, an imprint of Disney Book Group. No part of
this book may be reproduced or transmitted in any form or by any means, electronic
or mechanical, including photocopying, recording, or by any information storage and
retrieval system, without written permission from the publisher. For information address
Disney • Lucasfilm Press, 1101 Flower Street, Glendale, California 91201.

**LIBRARY OF CONGRESS CATALOGING-IN-PUBLICATION DATA**

*This title was previously cataloged with the following information:*

Heddle, Jennifer.
 Star Wars Rebels : Sabine's art attack / by Jennifer Heddle ; illustrated by Stephane
Roux.
  p. cm. (World of reading ; Level 1)
Summary: Rebel Sabine takes on a cadre of stormtroopers and uses her artistic talent to
tag a TIE fighter.
1. Artists--Juvenile fiction.  2. Space warfare--Juvenile fiction.  3. Life on other planets
--Juvenile fiction.  4. Imaginary wars and battles--Juvenile fiction.
I. Roux, Stephane, ill.
[E]--dc23

                   2014947444

978-1-61479-365-6 (reinforced library bound edition)

**ABDO**
**Spotlight**
A Division of ABDO
abdopublishing.com

Meet Sabine.

She loves to paint.
She is an artist.

She is also a rebel.
She fights for what is right.

One night, Sabine ran
through Lothal.
She had to hide from
the troopers.

The troopers were from the
Empire.
Sabine did not like troopers.

Sabine found a lot of TIE
fighters.
The TIE fighters belonged
to the Empire.

Sabine took out her spray
can. She began to paint.
Two troopers found her.

Sabine painted a purple
bird on a TIE fighter.
That made the troopers
angry.

They told Sabine to stop.
They said they would shoot.
Sabine said, "Okay. Shoot!"

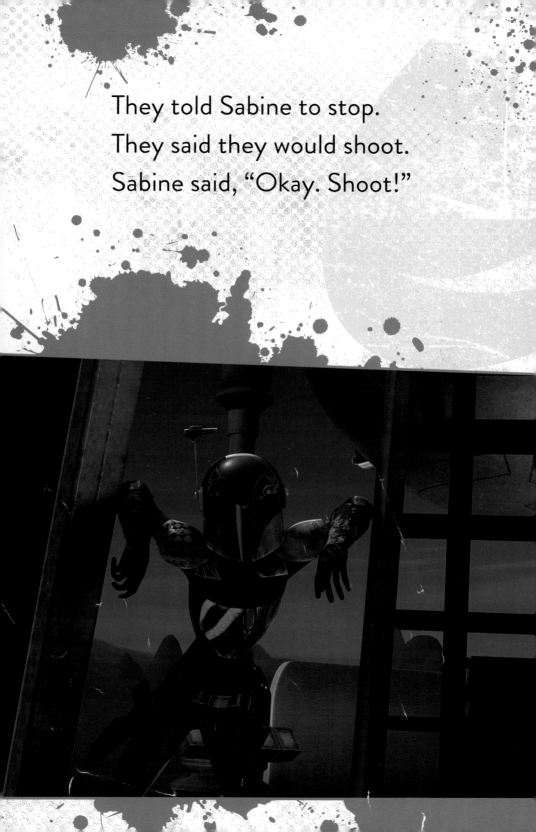

The troopers were confused.

Sabine ran away.

Sabine was good at
hiding. She was also
very fast.

The troopers tried to shoot her.
They always missed.

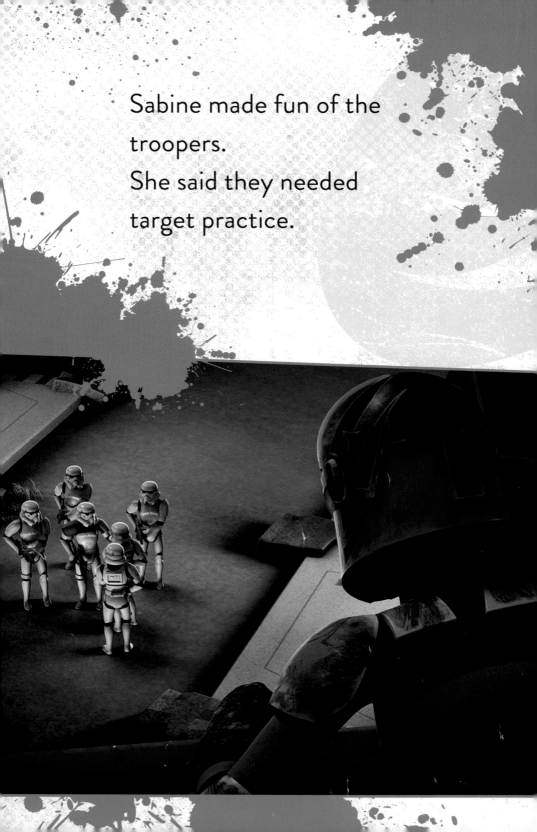

Sabine made fun of the
troopers.
She said they needed
target practice.

The troopers tried again
to hit Sabine.
They always missed.
She was too fast.

Sabine went back to her
painting.
It needed something
extra special.

Then a trooper found
her!
Sabine was in trouble!

19

Sabine kicked the
trooper in the leg.
The trooper fell.
Sabine ran away.

The other troopers looked
for Sabine.
They could not find her.

They looked at the painting
of the bird.
They saw something extra
special.

Sabine had added a bomb
to the painting!
Uh-oh!

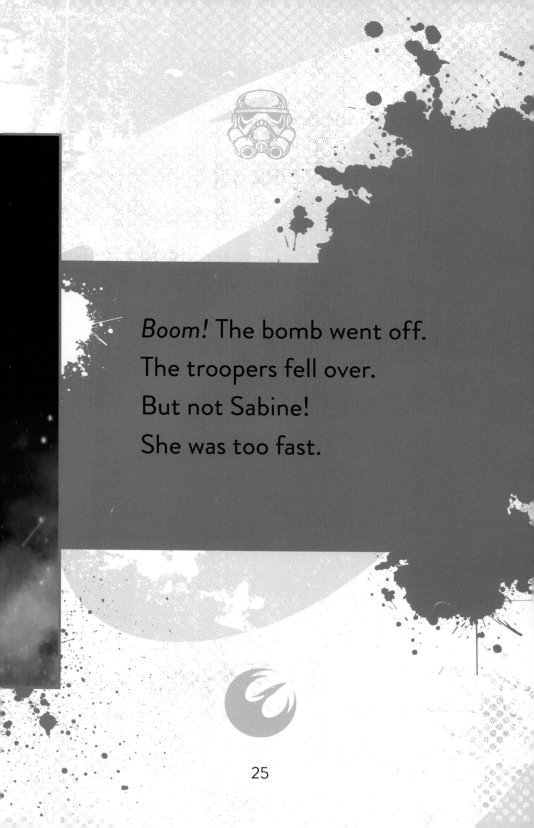

*Boom!* The bomb went off.
The troopers fell over.
But not Sabine!
She was too fast.

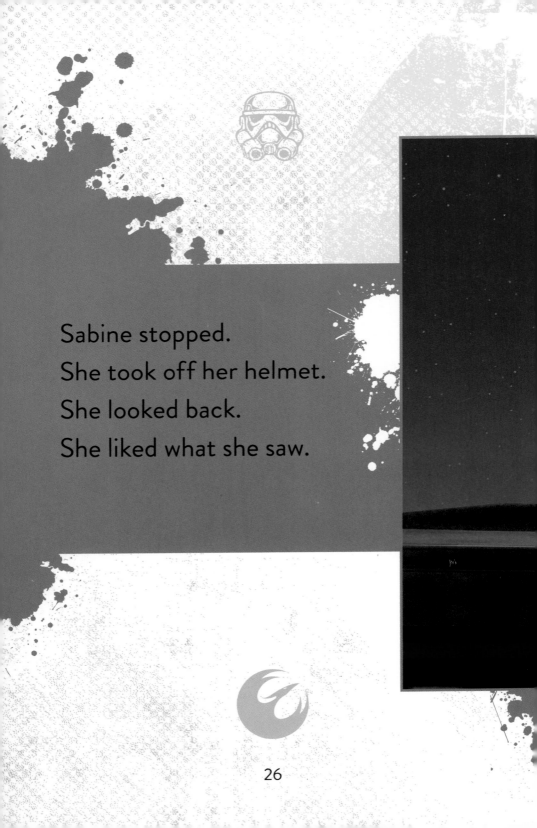

Sabine stopped.
She took off her helmet.
She looked back.
She liked what she saw.

The smoky sky was now a
pretty purple.

The bomb painted the
troopers purple, too!

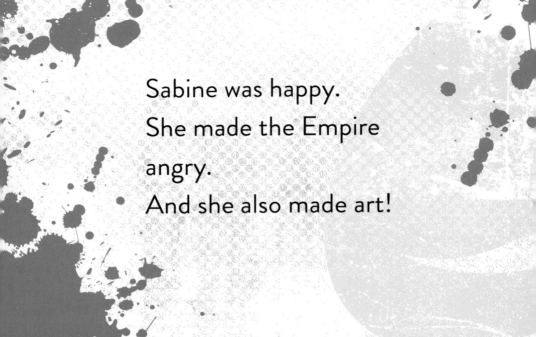

Sabine was happy.
She made the Empire
angry.
And she also made art!

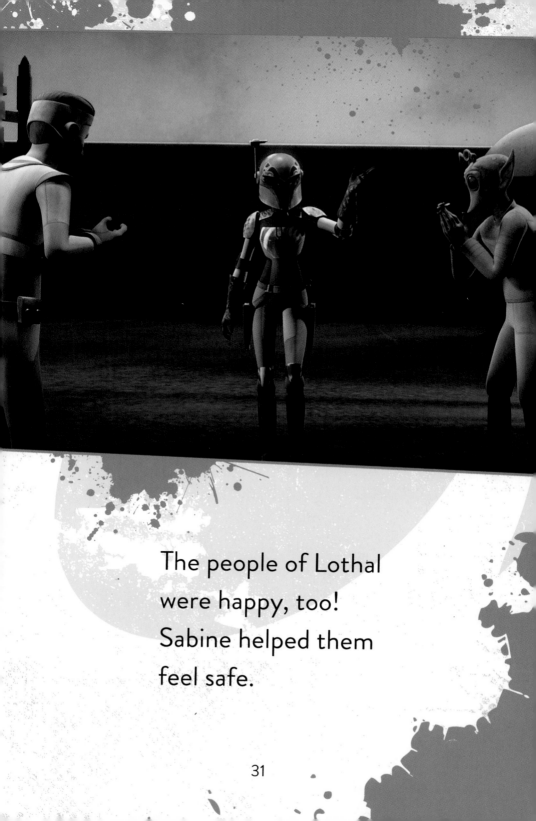

The people of Lothal
were happy, too!
Sabine helped them
feel safe.

Sabine is a rebel!